I0596504

ROSE MONTANA

The Experiment

Copyright © 2024 by Rose Montana

All rights reserved. No part of this publication may be reproduced, stored or transmitted in any form or by any means, electronic, mechanical, photocopying, recording, scanning, or otherwise without written permission from the publisher. It is illegal to copy this book, post it to a website, or distribute it by any other means without permission.

This novel is entirely a work of fiction. The names, characters and incidents portrayed in it are the work of the author's imagination. Any resemblance to actual persons, living or dead, events or localities is entirely coincidental.

Rose Montana asserts the moral right to be identified as the author of this work.

Book Cover Designed by: Rose Montana

First edition

This book was professionally typeset on Reedsy.
Find out more at reedsy.com

"The greatest seduction is the anticipation."

- Unknown

Contents

Foreword	ii
Prologue	1
Chapter 1	2
Chapter 2	6
Chapter 3	12
Chapter 4	14
Chapter 5	19
Chapter 6	21
Chapter 7	25
Chapter 8	35
Chapter 9	37
Chapter 10	50
Chapter 11	55
Chapter 12	58
Chapter 13	61
Chapter 14	65
Chapter 15	66
Chapter 16	71
Chapter 17	74
Chapter 18	75

Foreword

Trigger Warning

This is a dark romance - spicy taboo story.

Content and trigger warnings include: "forced" sex (meaning have to have sex every few days for government research) use of sex toys, descriptive sex scenes, no safe word allowed, CNC (consensual non-consent), MFM (male female male. Males don't interact), delayed orgasm, restraints/ being held down, disruption of a "scene", edging, and use of strong language.

Many will see this list and quickly turn to the next page, but please be advised: your mental health is important. If anything triggers you but still want to proceed, please do so with caution.

P.S. Mom or family, if you have found this book, please close it and put it down. Please... do not turn the page. You have been warned.

Prologue

Have you ever wondered, "I'm walking around as if everything is casual and fine, but no one knows I just had sex," or "I just had sex, but no one knows?" Well, I haven't had that experience. It's not because I haven't had sex, but because I've had so much sex, and everyone knows it. No, I'm not a slut sleeping around. It's because I live in a world where everyone— and I mean everyone—has sex, and everyone knows it.

Chapter 1

Hi, my name is Riley Reyes. I'm 23 and I live in the New World. It's the year 2195, and after China took over America, we became the New America. We live by China's rules, which determine almost every aspect of our lives, from where we live, what we eat, how we spend our free time, and, of course, population control. We are not allowed to reproduce, but as a human being with natural urges, our sex lives are studied closely and monitored by the government. The government determines when, where, and who we have sex with. They conduct sexual research to understand what triggers all types of arousal, and they claim this is to "save the human race." To carry out their research, they selected 250 men and women of "good breeding qualities" –in case their experiments go wrong and someone ends up pregnant. They conduct their research on us, forcing us into sex acts against our will. Some of these acts are fun, but others are far from enjoyable. Let me explain.

I've been in this community my whole life, but they start everyone off at age 16. I know, gross, but that's the world we live in now. Thankfully, it's not age 13 (insert cringe here). We all have our part to do, and when we do it, we're rewarded, but only after doing your part will everyone know. We are rewarded with either small gifts, a day off work, or an extra ration of dessert.

We are required to wear bracelets every day, and every time we finish our research session—called experiments—our bracelet glows until midnight. There are different colors for the type of experiment you were chosen to do.

With partner

- Orange–oral
- Blue–vaginal
- Purple–anal

With toys

- Red–dildo/vibrator
- Green–motor bunny
- White–fingers

And

- Pink–kink (whatever that is you learn more about once you hit 25 years of age).
- Silver–not called on yet
- Brown–failed/incomplete

There's no sense in trying to figure out how the colors correlate to the assignment. I've spent weeks trying to work it out—there's not much else to do here. Every day, we wake up, eat breakfast, and if you're under the age of 17, you go to school—yes, we have school. How else do you think I'd be able to write and tell you our history?

Anyways, we go to school until we turn 17, then we are moved to the workforce. There's no college—I think that's what the old world used to call it. We don't have anything like that. We don't have options to further our education. There aren't many jobs available. Everyone has to pick a job, whether they like it or not.

We have farmers; we have an amazing system that the old world failed at. We have electricians because someone has to keep the lights on, right? We have handymen who can fix things around the communities. Scientists usually run the "experiment," and we have an abundance of teachers. Since "experiments" are required frequently throughout the week, someone has to cover for the ones who leave. There are at least three teachers per classroom for this reason. All the kids know and understand why their teachers are leaving and accept that one day, that'll be them.

Growing up, you learn about the world we live in by age five. We are taught "Sex Ed" at age ten, but it's different from the old way of "Hey, males, make sure you cover up and don't get a young girl pregnant." Our new version is "Everyone, we live in the New World, separated from other communities—there are three other communities, as we've been told. In our community, they experiment to find out the science behind sex. We will be the community that eventually repopulates the world once it's safe again. So, we're gonna have you start having sex at age 16, and we'll monitor you as you grow. Fun right? Not really."

We are required to do experiments roughly three times a week, but it can vary depending on the need for research. Our bracelets will alert us by flashing or begin to beep if you don't hit the button "respond" in a given amount of time. When your bracelet alerts you, you head to the science "experiment" corridor, where they will bring you in and attach you to monitors. The scientist will instruct you on what you'll be doing that day. If you're

4

with a partner, you'll meet them, strip them, and then do the experiment. By your first year or two, you'll have experimented with every one of the opposite gender in your community.

The scientists' goal is to see what attraction there is between all genders and acts. In school, they taught us about the history of the old world: Male-Male, Male-Female, Female-Female, and even mixing up with multiple partners. As you grow older, they will begin to mix up your companions.

At age 25, they start you back in school, learning about the next round of "experiments." I've been told once you hit 26, they add in either an additional female or a male —to be honest, I'm nervous about that. There's something called DP. It's only ever been abbreviated, so I honestly don't know what it means, and I'm a little scared to know.

I have two more years of the first level of "experiments" and work. Oh, speaking of work, it's time for me to go. I'm a handyman—or handywoman, in my case—and I have to go fix things.

Chapter 2

Today was exhausting, I was in charge of fixing a window, a toilet–not fun I know—and a bed frame. I didn't ask what happened with the bed frame, but we all know. This is shocking because it's against the rules to have sex outside of the "experiments." They want to be able to capture it all. I'm surprised this hasn't been reported to the law. They can get reprimanded and punished–no one truly knows what happens when someone is reprimanded. The gossip I have heard is that they have been escorted out of our community and moved to Community One or Two, which is scary since we are known as the "chill" community. The others are relentless in their punishments and everyday life.

Today while working, I was paired with a guy who I've experimented with multiple times before, his name is Will Davis. He lives in a different sector of our community. We have up to fifty different sectors or sections based on age, sex, race, and even job. Will is filling in today for Roney, the usual boy I am paired with for work.

My mind flashes back to today's work,

"Hey, I'm Will," he states as he approaches me at our job board.

"Yeah, I remember. Do you know my name?" I tease.

He ponders for a second. His eyes rest a little higher than mine. He must be around six foot two compared to my five foot ten.

"Is it...Jade?" He asks with a snicker, as his lips form a smirk.

"No," I laugh, watching as his soft, brown eyes glimmer in the light.

"Is it...Juniper?"

"Not even close."

"Ugh, I give up, what's your name?" As he runs his hands through his short, brown hair.

"Wait, you're telling me we've had sex, and you don't remember my name? How rude!" I scoff, trying to hold back a laugh.

"Hey, I have a lot of sex," he laughs out. Dimples form as he smiles at me.

"Are you gloating?"

"No, why would I do that?"

"To attract me," I laugh.

"I have other ways of attracting you, but no, really, what's your name? I'm sorry I forgot."

"It's Riley."

"Yes! Riley, that's it. Well, again, I'm Will," he says, repeating himself.

"I know Wil...l," I stretch out the last "l".

We both burst into a fit of laughter.

—

Later when we were fixing the bed frame, Will breaks the silence asking, "So, what do you think they did here?"

"I think you know what happened."

"Do I?" he jokes, "Tell me what you think."

"Hmm..." I ponder. "I think she met him at work or on her way to work."

"How do you know it's a guy?" He cuts in.

"Why wouldn't it be?" I shoot back.

"Well, you know the old history."

"Okay, fair, but how do you explain that," I point to what looks like a white stain on the bed frame.

"Ew, I'm not touching that. Okay, you were saying she met HIM." He emphasizes "at work."

"Yes, they met at work, started hitting it off, and it grew into an affection. Even love...eeee." Will mimics throwing up.

"They wanted to have sex and not be monitored by everything and everyone. And they both enjoyed it," I finish my story.

"How do you know she enjoyed it?" He asks, throwing it back at me with a smile.

I simply point to another stain on the mattress

"Fair point. Wow, you're way too observant."

"I know, it's a blessing and a curse."

"But, are you sure that's how it truly happened," he starts up.

"Well, what else would have happened? The evidence is quite literally right there," I ask as I point back and forth at the stains.

"Well, let's say they did meet at work, but instead of them falling in love, they just simply wanted a good fuck without probing eyes and monitors."

"Wow, way to put no emotion into it."

"Because there was none."

I smile and chuckle at myself as we finish our project.

A beeping sound pulls me out of my memory of today. Looking around, I see my bracelet is flashing and now beeping. I groan knowing it's my turn for that time of day. Putting my journal down and sliding on my slip-ons—I only wear these when I have to take them off quickly— I glance at the small mirror I have in my sparse bedroom, giving myself a mental nod of approval as I head out the door.

Walking down the long hall is always nerve-racking. You have no clue what your assignment is till you walk into the room. Will I be by myself, with a toy, or with a partner today?

Coming upon the black, ominous door, I hear voices on the other side as I wrap my knuckles four times. Knock. Knock. Knock, pause. Knock— it's the specific code you're supposed to give them when you're coming in—the door opens as a rush of cold air hits my skin. I don't know why. I always forget it's cold here. Maybe it's because I'm usually sweating by the time I leave.

Walking in, I see the scientist. The scientists are always different, I never bother to learn their names. Today in the room stands two scientists and a boy. I don't recognize this boy. He looks young, really young, beginner young.

"Oh, good you're here," says one of the scientists, looking at me.

"Yeah, sorry I got caught up," I lie.

She waves her hand, dismissing my statement. "That's fine. We were introducing Sean here to everything in the room." Sean looks scared—no, correction, frightened. Throwing on a cheery smile, I stretch out my hand, and he just stares at it.

"Hi, I'm Riley," again, he just stares with horror.

"Sorry, this is his first time," a scientist tells me.

That explains the timidness. Man, I barely remember my first time. It was so long ago. Wait, that means this kid is 16 and I'm 23 Wow! I don't think I've ever been someone's first before. Now, I'm nervous.

The scientist explains the process once more to Sean, as I look around the room. The scientist steps toward him to show him the monitors and he flinches, hard enough he falls backward, knocking over the medical table with all the supplies.

We are going to be here for a while. Usually, they hook us up, have us do the deed, and then leave. I think we've been here for a half hour already. When Sean finally calms down, I reach over and place my hand on his arm.

"Hey, it's okay. It's not as bad as you'd think. Honestly, you guys have it easy. You just have to move. It's us girls that have to deal with the pain and the blood."

"Blood?" he shrieks.

"Only the first time girls bleed. I've been doing this for six years. You're going to be okay." He relaxes, only slightly.

"Okay, let's begin," the scientist states. "It will be low impact and energy. I'll have you both strip and to start, Riley, I'll have you lie on your back on the bed and Sean I'll have you climb over her."

Sean's eyes widen when she mentions the word "strip."

I'm so used to this now, that I don't bother going behind the privacy curtain, but Sean does. He comes out a few minutes later shaking as though he is cold to the bone.

The scientists start to coax him out from behind the privacy curtain, like coaxing a baby deer out of the woods. Walking over to the scientist, I get set up with the monitors and wait for Sean to get set up. I take the initiative and hop on the bed, lying down fully exposed. Sean comes around and faces me. He freezes and his eyes bug out when he sees me fully exposed, sprawled out on the bed. His body begins to react exactly how it should. I see his erection harden quickly.

"Well, there we go," says one of the scientists. "Sean, please climb on top of Miss Riley, and we'll begin." Sean walks sheepishly over and climbs on top of me.

"I'm sorry, I'm nervous. But you're beautiful," he tells me, through chattering teeth.

"Thank you."

"Okay, Sean, we need you to put your penis into her vagina."

"What?" As though he's forgotten all their instructions and what we do in this room.

Rolling my eyes, I grab hold of his dick and direct it where to go. I can feel him hardening even more under my fingers.

"Right there. Now push it in and thrust in and out of me," I order him.

"Oh...okay." He moves his hips forward, shoving his cock into me. He isn't long by any means, but he does have some width to him. A moan slips out of me as he starts to move in and out of me slowly. Painfully slowly, almost too slow.

"I...I think I got it," he stumbles out.

"Good, now go faster," I plainly state.

"Ok!" He states excitedly, getting the hang of it.

He starts to slide his penis in and out at a faster pace, but not long after he starts to move, he freezes.

"What's wrong?" I ask.

"Oh no," he says, scared, and then a second later I feel it. He comes inside me.

"Well, that was..." one scientist starts.

"Quick," says the other, "okay, time to clean everyone up."

I leave the room with a brown bracelet, and Sean glows with blue. I didn't come, meaning I failed my "experiment". I head back to my room, in a walk of shame.

Chapter 3

For the next few days, I'm in a slump. I go to work, go home, and repeat, getting called in only once. On the fifth day after my failed experiment, I head into work and see Will waiting by the job board.

"Where's Roney?" I ask.

"Sick. Again," he states.

"Dang, I hope I don't catch what he has." Especially since no one gets sick here, if he's actually sick, then we're all screwed.

"Me neither."

"Hey, how'd your experiment go the other day?" he questions.

"Ugh, don't remind me of that."

"Not good, huh?"

"Nope. I left with a brown."

"Ouch, that'll reflect badly on you."

"Yeah, thankfully two days ago, I was assigned a toy they picked out and was by myself. So I left with a glowing red bracelet."

"That's great!"

"Yeah, how have your experiments been?"

"Fine."

"Just fine?" You have to give me more than that."

"Ugh, they're filling in spots with new people and I get it, we were all new once, but yesterday a young girl cried. I got her off, but she cried and screamed through the whole thing."

"Yikes!"

"Yeah," he kicks an invisible rock. "Oh, well, we all have to learn how to do it. " He goes quiet after that.

When we head to our assigned job location, I watch him start to work for a few minutes, tinkering with the tools in his hands. I bet you he would be great at the fingering portion. Whoa! Where did that thought come from?

"Riley?" He says my name in a sing-song tone. Crap - I was staring at him as I zoned out.

"Yes, sorry what?"

"Hand me the flathead screwdriver, please."

"Sure." Clearing my throat, I pass him the tool, shaking my head at those thoughts.

Chapter 4

The next day, I'm called into the "experiment" early, the alarm waking me up. Weird. I've never been called in this early. Still in my pajamas, I throw on my slip-on shoes as I head out the door. I stopped short when I saw that the black door was already cracked open. I grip my hand around the edge of the door and pull it open the rest of the way when I see Will.

"Will?" I ask, surprised.

"Hey, Riley."

"What are you doing here?"

"I'm here for the "experiment." I got called in, and clearly, so did you."

"Oh, yeah. Duh," I let out a sheepish chuckle.

The scientist runs through the instructions, as usual, but compared to the past when we had intercourse, they're having him finger me today.

I'm nervous and I don't know why. Again, I've done this "experiment" hundreds of times before, so I should not be nervous. Maybe it's because I had just imagined him being good with his fingers. Yes, maybe that is why.

We slowly slip out of our clothes, getting attached to the machines, as I climb onto the bed, but before he can climb over me the scientist interjects,

"Wait!"

"What?" We both ask in unison, pausing.

"Switch positions."

"What?" We ask again.

"Riley, you will be on top and Will, you will be on bottom."

"Will this work?" I ask.

"Yes," the scientist pauses and looks up at us. "We've been expanding our research and we're going to test it out."

"Okay..."

We do as she instructed. I jump off the bed, and Will climbs up to lie down. I climb and straddle his body, unsure where I should sit. Will grabs hold of my hips pulling me towards his waist and planting me down right above his cock. I feel the warmth of his body radiating from him and his cock tapping at my back end, as I shift on him to get comfortable. Both of our machines start rapidly beeping, knowing our heart rates are racing.

"Okay, now that you are on top, Riley. Will, we want you to rub her clit instead of inserting your fingers."

He nods, moving his fingers towards my clit. I lean back a bit, giving him more access, as I place my hands on his legs to support myself. He starts by slowly tapping my clit. I start to moan and move my hips back and forth. I hear faint scribbles of pencils to paper from their analysis. My head falls back as a sharp gasp escapes my lips. Bringing my head back up, I glance down at Will as he holds a smirk to his smile. Oh no, what is he planning?

His circles get smaller, but faster. Oh my god, fuck. I'm caught off guard when a scientist interjects my pleasure, "Riley, try not to move."

Shit. Why? It's going to be hard to sit still. I feel his cock behind me, hitting my lower back with every movement he makes. With sudden movements, Will quickly stops his circles, grabs hold of my hips, lifts me, places me back down a second later, and begins his circles again. I'm confused only for a brief second when I realize what he did. He lifted me to slide his cock underneath me. I can feel his cock hardening and I'm not sure what the feeling is but, I want him... I want him to insert it in me. He continues rubbing my clit, a mix of small and large circles.

"OH, MY GOD! FUCK!" I scream out. As the scientists' pencils race along their papers.

Before I have a second thought, I am coming. And coming HARD. I collapse on top of his body and I feel his cock throbbing underneath my stomach. Oh my god, I want him to fuck me right now. I want to feel his hard cock inside me as he pulses and releases his pleasure. I want to make out with him—that's one thing we don't do during the "experiments." I've never been kissed—my breath is hard and deep. I can feel his breathing is the same, though I'm not sure if he came or not.

Raising my head, I look at him. His eyes are soft, and he holds a cheeky grin on his face as beads of sweat race down the side of his face.

"Perfect!" one of the scientists exclaims, pulling our attention away from each other. I sit up only to discover he did come, and it's half on me and half on him.

We clean ourselves up and get dressed. Both of our bracelets are bright white. After cleaning up, we are sent on our way. Once the door closes behind us, we stand there speechless.

"What was..." I start.

"That?" He finishes for me

"I'm not sure, but can I say something?" I ask.

"Of course," he says, almost sounding breathless.

"I've never kissed anyone, but during the "experiment." I

wanted to kiss you."

"Same," he bluntly says.

"Should we?" I half-jokingly ask.

"No, it's against the rules," he states.

"Right."

We both stand there for a few seconds longer. When he takes a step in the opposite direction, only to turn a complete 180 degrees, he kisses me. His lips connect to mine fiercely. A sharp inhale of air, as I'm caught by surprise. I can't breathe. I only mimic what he does with his lips. He tastes so good! Is that weird to say? I don't care. The feeling rushes through me, the same feeling I had during our "experiment." I feel like a virgin again, experiencing things for the first time.

His hand comes up to cup my face as his lips are still connected to mine. His hand moves along my chin, neck, and down to my breasts. Sensations rush through my body, sensations I haven't experienced before. I want more, but I don't know how. I'm new at this. I've only done what they've told me to do. Has he done more? Has he done this before? This pulls me out of the moment. I stop abruptly, and he stops too.

"You okay?" he asks, breathless.

"Yeah, I just thought I heard someone," I lie.

"Oh. Wow, I don't know what that was."

"Me neither, but I liked it."

"Me too!"

We're both smiling at each other when there is movement from around the corner. It sounds like footsteps.

"Oh...hey man, how are you doing?" a guy, maybe in his twenties, asks Will.

Will's cheeks flush bright red, but trying to cover it up, he responds, "Good. I am just living."

"Yup. I got my call to come in. Curious what they'll have me do today?" the man says, chuckling.

I didn't think Will's cheeks could get any redder, but they do. I can tell he's thinking about what they had us do and maybe also our kiss.

"Yeah, good luck, man," Will states.

"Thanks, but I won't need it," the man says as he walks through the black door.

We both burst into laughter.

—

Later that night, I lie awake, thinking about that kiss. His fingers are on me, making me come only from rubbing my clit. My hand moves down to my clit. I've never touched myself there outside of the "experiments," but tonight, I am thinking not only of him and what we did but the possibilities of what we could do.

Chapter 5

The next few days fly by as work seems to only get busier. Roney is back from being sick. I guess he had something called the flu, which is new in the New World. He said it knocked him out for a few days, and then he was fine as though nothing happened. He asked if anything interesting happened while he was out sick. I tried my best to hide my blushing cheeks but only told him about the broken bed frame and the theory Will and I had.

Roney burst out laughing. "You know," he says, "that's been happening a lot more lately."

"Really?" I questioned.

"Oh, yeah. I guess the scientist got tired of the same old, same old "experiments", so they're switching things up. I haven't experienced the new "experiments", but I'm intrigued now. Have you?"

"Have I what?" I ask, caught off guard.

"Have you had to do the new "experiment"?"

I feel my face flushing with embarrassment. The memory of Will getting me off by rubbing my clit and then our kiss afterward sends heat rushing through my body.

"Nope," I rush out.

"Oh, okay," he says, shrugging.

Does he know? No, how would he?

The day progresses after that. There are no new orders to fix broken windows, bed frames, or much of anything. Roney and I are sent home early due to the lack of work, which I gladly take. As I make it to my room with my key in the keyhole, my bracelet starts to flash. Of course.

Spinning on my heels, I turn around and head towards the "experiment" room. Knocking on the door with the four required knocks, I wait and wait. No one opens the door. I knock again and wait. Again, no response.

Well, that's weird. Knocking a third time, I place my hand on the doorknob, only to find it locked.

I don't think this door has ever been locked. No one wants to come here; we're only required to do so.

I start to pace in front of the door, giving them a few minutes. Maybe my bracelet chimed before they were done with the last session. Nodding to myself, I decide to wait a little longer.

After ten minutes with no sound of anyone being inside, I decide to leave. But as I step around the corner, I hear the creak of the door opening. Curiosity gets the better of me. Not wanting whoever is walking out to see me, I plaster myself along the wall and slowly peek around the corner.

There is a boy, who can't be much older than Will and a girl. I can't seem to place the boy's name, but the girl looks familiar. How? They are whispering to one another and both of their hair is a mess. In between their whispers, they are breathing heavily, as though they just did an hour-long workout in the tiny room. As the girl turns slightly to the left, I see the girl's cheeks are flushed bright red.

Did they have unauthorized sex?

Chapter 6

Later that night, I recount what I saw in the hall. I'm almost certain they had unauthorized sex, but why in there? And how did my bracelet get triggered?

Deciding I won't be able to sleep tonight, I head out of my room and slip into a common area. There are a few people scattered around, but all are separated from one another. I notice one of the women playing cards. Her normal wavy blond hair is brushed out, making her hair look straight. She is known to be a gossiper and the perfect person I want to talk to this evening. Sliding in the chair across from her, I start up a conversation.

"Hey, Allison, got a question for you?" I begin.

"Draw."

"What?"

"Draw a card. Do you want to get caught?"

"No?" I ask, concerned.

"Then draw and ask your question," I draw eight cards, laying two down when I have a pair, then draw two more.

"What have you heard about the new "experiments"?"

"What new "experiments"?"

"Don't give me that. I know you hear it all."

She looks up through her eyelashes at me, then shoots her eyes around the room to see if anyone else is listening.

Leaning in, she starts, "I've heard the government was getting the same inconclusive results for the old "experiments," and when someone found an Old World textbook on the "Facts of Pleasure," they decided to test those theories out."

"Facts of pleasure? So they're not just testing for how sex triggers activates, and affects our minds, they're now testing for pleasure? What exactly is pleasure?" I ask her.

She looks at me like I've grown two heads. "You silly girl. Have you ever touched yourself down there, outside of the "experiments," of course, and felt a rush, a heat, and a weird sensation?"

"Touched myself? There?" I question, "I've only done what they've instructed in the rooms."

She shakes her head, tisking. "You poor girl. Have you been fingered or had your clit rubbed during the "experiments"?"

"Yeah, multiple times," my mind tries not to flashback to the last time with Will.

"Okay, so you do that, but with yourself."

"Yes, in the room, with scientists instructing me, but I've never felt that sensation you're referring to."

She groans, "That's because you're doing it for the tests but not physically enjoying it. Not enjoying the pleasure. You are doing it to cum, and only that. But if you do it yourself, and push past the cum and continue to pleasure yourself, then you will feel and enjoy true Pleasure."

Shaking my head, I said, "No, it's against the rules; I could get punished."

She burst out laughing. "Punished. Oh, silly girl, they say that so you won't take away from their "experiment", but it's only an empty threat. They won't punish you, just don't get caught. Do it early in the morning or late in the evening, when you're supposed to be sleeping. Pleasure is that feeling rushing through your body, and once you finish, your body feels good, relaxed, and happy. That's the real way all of us females are supposed to feel after the "experiments."

"Have you done the new "experiment?" I ask her.

"Oh, no, honey, I've aged out."

"Aged out? I thought that was a myth," I ask incredulously.

"Yes, once you hit 35, they age you out, thinking you're not fresh enough. That's why I pleasure myself. Have you?"

"No," I lie again, "I was supposed to have a session today, but something weird happened."

"Weird, how?" She sits up straighter in her seat.

I decide to tell her about what I saw, and with each detail, her eyes grow wider and wider.

"I bet you they were having unauthorized sex in there."

"That's what I thought too."

"It's more common than you think."

"That's what I've been hearing lately, but are you sure?"

"Oh, for sure. With all the emotions running high after the "experiments," it's no wonder we're all not pregnant."

A yawn escapes me while I mumble out, "Wow."

"You should go to bed, dear. I'll keep what we talked about quiet. You go to rest, and if you get back and you can't sleep, try pleasuring yourself."

"Thank...s," I say, drawing out the word.

Back in my room, I lie awake thinking all of what she said. Deciding to give it a try, I move my hand down underneath the elastic band of my sweatpants and feel the warmth of my skin. This is weird, I think, yanking my hand out of my pants. Turning over, I try to go to sleep again. After a few more minutes pass and no sleep comes, I slide my hand back down my pants and feel around to where Will touched me.

My stomach tightens at the thought, but I don't stop. It feels awkward and uncomfortable at first, but then I start to rub small circles on my clit and freeze when I feel a rush of tingling trails through my body. This is usually where I cum in the "experiments" and stop, but instead, I begin to explore more. I think about Will and his body. His cock under my pussy and how desperate I was for it. Desperately wanting him to fuck me.

I slide a finger between my folds. I feel I am already wet. Rubbing and moving my fingers in and out of my body. I let out a moan without intending to. Breathing heavily, I think about Will again, touching me, even when his hands gripped my waist, lifting me to move his cock underneath me. I continue to form circles around my clit, as another moan, this one a little louder than before, escapes my lips as I reach the peak, and a rush of ecstasy floods through me. My body relaxes, and a sense of calm coats my body.

Breathing heavily, I pull my hand away, covered in my wetness, and settle into bed. Sleep takes me under a second later.

Chapter 7

A few days later, I start my day like any other: get up, get ready for work, and then head into work when a flashing light comes from my wrist. Wondering if this is accurate this time, I let Roney know I'm being called in for an "experiment."

"Alright! Have fun," he yells back to me as I drop my tools off at the toolbox and head towards the "experiment" room. Before I can leave the section I'm in, Will comes running up to me.

"Hey, where are you headed?" he asks.

I point down at my bracelet.

"Ahh," he remarks, chuckling.

"What's so funny?" I ask.

"Oh, nothing..."

"No, tell me. Wait, where are you going?" Realizing he is headed in the same direction as me.

He smiles and holds up his wrist to his bracelet flashing. No way!

"Really?" I ask.

"Yes, it started a minute ago."

"But, we were just paired together. They never pair us up again until full rotation is done."

"I don't know," he shrugs. "Wait, do you not want to do it with me again?"

I shove his arm. "Oh...stop, you know what I mean."

"He laughs, and we walk towards the "experiment" room door together.

We reach the black door, Will jumps in front of me to knock first, laughing. After he knocks four times, the door opens, and I pause to see who's on the other side. The girl from a few days ago, who might have had unauthorized sex, but today she is put together with not a hair out of place.

"Welcome back, you two," she says in a cheery tone, smiling.

"So sorry, Riley, about the other day's mix-up. The machine malfunctioned, and we had to shut the whole system down, so no one was called in. We are now behind in our research," she adds under her breath.

She's either lying through her teeth, or maybe she is telling the truth, but she knew no one would be coming around and took advantage of it.

"That's okay. I figured something happened by mistake when the door was locked. But I'm wondering why we are both here again today. Don't you normally switch up partners?" I look between Will and the girl.

"Oh, yes, but we reviewed the results from the other day, and both of you showed a high neurotransmitter level and significantly increased hormone levels. We wanted to bring you in again to see if it was a fluke or real."

Will and I look at one another skeptically.

"So, what are we doing today?" Will interjects, changing the subject.

"We are doing something brand new!" She says, almost giddy.

That has me worried.

"Okay, first, let's have you guys strip and get hooked up to monitors," she says.

We both undress, remove our work outfits and place them in neat piles on the opposite side of the room. Then, we head over to the monitors to be hooked up. Glancing at Will, I see he has his eyes closed, perhaps mentally preparing himself.

Once we're both hooked up, the girl claps her hands and begins, "Okay! Today, I want Riley on the bed."

"Okay," I say, starting to climb up, placing my head at the far end and lying down.

"No, Riley, we need you closer to the end of the bed."

"Closer?" I question.

"Yes, bring your butt at the edge of the bed."

"Okay..." I scoot down, feeling uneasy and off balance. "Where do I place my feet?" I ask.

"You'll wrap them around Will's body."

Will and I make eye contact and stare at one another in shock.

"Now, Will, walk over to the edge of the bed, aligning your pelvis with Riley's. Let her wrap her legs around you and let her body pull you closer."

Will takes a hesitant step forward, aligning himself as instructed. I wrap my legs around his waist, feeling the awkwardness of the situation intensify. I can feel the heat radiating off his body and his cock nearing my opening. If I were to move my hips forward, I could tease him into entering me. Flashbacks from last night when I touched myself flood my memory as my skin heats up and my head begins to feel dizzy. He inches closer as the scientist approaches to adjust the monitors attached to us.

"Let's start," the scientist says, "Will, I want you to do what you did last time. Begin by rubbing circles around her clit, varying the speed and circle size."

"Riley, go ahead and get comfortable. Your hands can either

be on your stomach or off to the side," she says, going back to check the monitors.

Will starts, catching me off guard as the tingling sensation begins to fill my body. Damn, this feels so good. He begins with slow, large circles and then switches to smaller, quick circles. My body is overwhelmed with sensations right now.

"Riley, remember to breathe," the scientist says. Realizing I haven't taken a break in a minute.

"Now, Will, start stroking your cock with your free hand."

"What?" We both question in unison.

"Just do it, Will."

Hesitantly, Will takes his free hand and moves his cock above my vaginal opening, beginning to stroke himself. He matches the speed of the circles he's making on my clit, to the movement of him slowly stroking up and down his shaft. He increases the speed of the circles on my clit, as his strokes rapidly increase. I find myself wishing I was the one stroking his cock. Whoa! What? I have never done that. My body temperature has been increasing with each touch. He's hot, and I love what he's doing to me, but am I starting to have feelings towards Will?

As I lay there, close to the edge of the bed, with Will's hand rubbing me and his other hand stroking himself, I slightly turned my head to the side to watch him better. I see his erection continuing to harden in his hands. When he pulls his hand back down his shaft, I notice a small amount of glistening liquid at the tip. A deep longing flows through me — I want to taste it, to lick it up, and if there's more, I want it.

"Now," the scientist begins, pulling me away from my imagination. "Will, when you're ready, insert your cock, hard, into her."

He shoots a look up at her. "Wait?"

"Just shove it in, trust me," she says with an unsettling level of enthusiasm. She must enjoy her job. Can you imagine watching hundreds of people have sex every day while still recording it? I glance back at her, and she nods vigorously, her voice becoming a blur as if I have cotton balls in my ears.

"What?" I asked, sounding confused.

"He's going to thrust himself into you forcefully, and trust me, it will feel amazing! Might be a little painful at first, but it will be a new sensation," she says, this with her eyes closed and a bright, full smile on her face.

Will looks at me hesitantly. I freeze, unsure of what to do. I'm not allowed to say "no," or the entire test will end, and I will fail again— probably dragging Will down with me. I can't afford another failure this month. I have already been penalized by getting more shifts added to my work schedule—I'm still enjoying the sensations flowing through me from his fingers and watching him stroking himself.

"Umm..." I begin, not fully realizing what I'm about to say.

"Do it, Will. She will enjoy it," the scientist says.

I have had hundreds of dicks inside me but none where they're forcefully shoved into me, by instructions. I feel my pussy clench with that thought as a sickening feeling fills my stomach. Will it hurt? If so, how bad?

Will looks between me and the scientist, clearly unsure. I nod, giving him a signal that it's okay and he can proceed. I can see Will is still grappling with doubts and uncertainties, much like I am.

With a deep breath in from both of us, he takes a half step backward, angeling and lining himself at my entrance. He knocks his cock between my lips, and I gasp inwardly, anticipating the moment. I can feel the small amount of precum that was sitting on top of his head, knowing now his precum is on me. The thought of him doing this, in this manner, and the possibilities send a lightning bolt through me. I hadn't realized he had stopped touching my clit and is now watching me.

"Will, you have to continue touching her, continue to rub her clit, even tease her a bit."

"Tease her?" he asks.

"Don't fully insert your finger, but rub your finger in her folds."

Will begins the curves again, elongated curves. One of his fingers continues circling as another one starts to rub the lips of my pussy.

"Fuck!" I shout. I can feel myself getting wetter by the second.

"Will," the scientist starts, "once her pussy becomes wet, you can shove your cock into her."

"Okay..." Will says, only continuing to rub me.

"Oh, just shove it in. If you go too slow, it won't have the right effect."

His eyes widen to the size of saucers, looking between the way too-eager scientist and me. Looking for approval from both of us. When his gaze meets mine, I can see he's trying to apologize. I close my eyes slowly, take a deep breath, and nod, bracing myself for the impact. I have had a lot of sex, ranging from virgin sex to more playful sex before, but nothing like this, nothing so forceful. Opening my eyes, I see Will is still watching me.

Taking another deep breath, he moves his hips backward and then thrusts into me hard. I let out a sharp breath.

"OH MY GOD!" I scream and moan, but Will doesn't stop, freeze, or react. He only continues with his hard fucking. I don't know if the scientist told him what to do or if he's doing it on instinct, but he is thrusting himself in and halfway out of me before forcefully shoving his cock in me. The sensation from my clit, combined with the feeling of him moving in me, overwhelms my senses. My body reacts instinctively, unable to fully describe the intensity. It's a mix of amazing and euphoric, a sensation unlike anything I've ever felt before. His cock is long, touching my cervix with each thrust. I fear he will pass my cervix and cause damage.

A few wonderful and sensational minutes go by in between me moaning, gasping, and yelling, "FUCK!" My hands have found their way to grasping the bed as though my life depended on it.

Continuing to pound me into the bed. Each time his penis pulls out of my body, it feels as though something is missing, only to slam back into me, filling up the space. A sharp exhale, and a loud moan leaves my lips. I'm not sure when I reclosed my eyes, but opening them, I looked up to see Will. He's focused, sweat drips down his face, and he's not looking at me but almost through me. I attempt to move my hand to touch him, to feel him, but when attempting to move my hand upward, his hand, the one that was on my clit, catches my hand and pins it to the bed.

I hear a slight gasp come from the scientist, it was delayed—due to maybe her concentration on the monitors, or perhaps she was entranced in our movements. I'm not sure.

"Will," she begins, but then stops and lets him continue his hard thrusts.

"Will," I start, but I don't think Will can see me. He's so focused.

"Will!" I say a little louder. His hand is now tightly wrapped around my wrist and begins to hurt where he's holding it down. He is still thrusting into me, but I only feel the movement now.

I want him to stop. I need him to stop. I'm no longer enjoying myself, but he continues to thrust into me, his thrusts increasing speed and pain.

"Will..." My voice breaks, saying his name again.

Suddenly, Will freezes

"Will?" I ask softly.

"I...I'm about to come," he croaks out.

I shoot a look at the scientist in a quick motion, shaking her, "Okay, Will pull out of her. Now!"

He's focused, listening, and with one more thrust into me, he pulls out as fast. Cold air instantly contacts my now exposed skin, making me crave his cock back in me. Why did I want him to stop again? I wonder to myself. He stands, releasing my wrist and backing away as my legs fall against the bed. I see he is still holding onto his cock, slowly stroking it, keeping it erect.

"Okay," the scientist starts again. We want her to come first this time, and then you can come. " A groan leaves Will's throat.

"Riley, dear, how are you feeling?" She asks.

"I feel...pretty good, a little shaken up," I say, trying not to meet Will's glance.

"Okay, do you think you're close to coming?" She asks, hopeful.

"I don't know, I'm not sure, honestly," I say sheepishly.

"That's okay, Will," she looks towards Will, "I will have you finish off Riley. I want you to continue with her clit, then when she starts getting wet again, move a finger or two into her. Your choice."

My body clenches. Not only has he played with my clit, he fucked me hard, and now he's going to finger fuck me. I wonder what color my bracelet will be after this today. Rainbow?

Will pulls me out of my thoughts as he takes a few steps close to me. I freeze, hesitant, then moving his hand down to my clit, he starts to tease. He immediately starts circles, then tapping, then again back to fast circles. I'm already aroused, so this won't last long.

"Holy shit!" I yell out, squirming on the bed. I raise my hand and grip his forearm, needing to do something with my hands other than grabbing at the bed again.

"Now!" the scientist exclaims. She might have said it in a normal tone, but to my ears, it sounded like a yell. Like the start of a race. NOW!

He shoves not one, not two, but three fingers into me. I rise fully into a seated position, resting on my elbows, and suck in a deep breath. He starts fingering me, moving his fingers back and forth, and before I know what's happening. My body clenches, and I come. Hard! Collapsing on my back, I let my pleasure roll through me as I close my eyes. Laying there for a few seconds, I peek at what he's doing. I see he is still stroking himself, but faster now, while his three fingers are still in me. Precum rests on top of his cock, starting to drip.

"Now, Will, you are allowed to come, but let Riley tell you where. Riley, tell him where you'd like him to come. You can say in his hand, on a towel, on you, or wherever you'd like, but not in you. We don't need any pregnancies to occur."

My eyes shoot open, "what?"

"Riley..." Will struggles to say my name. "Choose one."

"Umm..." my mind is racing a hundred miles.

"Riley.... please...I'm going to come," I look down to see there is more precum, or maybe it's now cum forming at the head of his cock.

"Uh... I don't know..."

"Ril..."

"On me. ON ME!" I shout!

He moves forward an inch, letting his body connect between my legs once again, and let his cock spray his cum all over my belly and chest. It is warm as it hits my skin. He groans and falls forward. It isn't until his labored breathing matches mine that I realize his fingers are still in me. He makes a few more moves, pulling them out, and I come again.

Chapter 8

We both lay there, breathing heavily, as the scientist makes her final notes on her clipboard. I don't know if she was writing during this entire interaction or if she was just coaching us. I can't think clearly. We both lay here, still. I wish the bed was big enough for both of us to lie on.

The bed, if that's what they call it, resembles more of a doctor's office bed, but it's comfier. It's smaller than a twin bed but can raise the headrest and the upper half of the bed. Plus, the whole system can be adjusted up or down. So, it's a more comfortable doctor's bed with an actual mattress.

The scientist starts to wave her hand in front of Will and I.

"Hey...I don't mean to rush, but we need to prepare the bed for the next couple. Here's a warm towel to clean yourselves up. I'd recommend cleaning your vagina, Riley, first, then cleaning up his cum and him. I'll give you two some space, but you have about five minutes. Sorry." Her smile is short as she exits the room.

After a minute, Will pushes himself up off me, and I feel it the moment his weight is gone. He grabs hold of the washcloth and starts to clean me up. I jump when the washcloth connects with my skin.

"Sorry. It cooled down."

"Yeah," he says shortly.

"Hey, are you okay?" I ask.

He doesn't respond; he only continues to clean me up.

"We need to hurry," is all he says when he finally does speak. We finish cleaning ourselves up and get dressed. As we're heading out the door, I stop.

"What is going on?"

"Nothing."

"No, not nothing. You seemed perfectly fine in there, and now you're mad."

"I'm fine," he spits out.

"No, you're not. Do not lie to me."

He starts to speak when our bracelets start to glow. Mine glows white and blue, while he glows white. It doesn't seem fair when he was fucking me when he was about to come, but they made him stop and finish off by stroking himself.

"Well, that's just great," he says.

"What?"

"I have to go."

"What the fuck?" I try to race after him, but he turns around and shouts, "Riley, please just leave me the fuck alone."

I stop short in my tracks. He's never spoken so sharply towards me before.

"Will...?"

He doesn't respond, only walks away with his fists hanging next to him. I continue to watch him as he turns the corner and vanishes from sight.

Chapter 9

Work is awkward with a capital A the next day. A large ventilation area in the third sector broke in the middle of the night, calling all available units to work on it—Roney and I, a few others, and Will and another girl. The girl is pretty, with pale skin and deep auburn hair. She's maybe five feet tall, five inches tall, and thin compared to my large size. Her eyes are a soft gray color, and I can tell she added lipstick to today's work attire.

Due to the ventilation breaking during the night, the air quality isn't as good as it should be. There is a higher risk of contamination in the air mixing with the outside world. Our bosses give us the rundown on the possible side effects that could arise: nausea, runny nose, dizziness, headaches, blackout, and if shit hits the fan, we lose feeling, our body will go cold, then we die.

The girl next to Will shrieks and goes pale. They also instructed us on a few things to do before we reached sector three. Make sure to drink plenty of water on the way up, and don't turn on your air masks unless you have to—there's only enough air per person to put the mask on and then get out.

We all make our way to the stairs, three flights up, straight. If you slip, you will fall straight down and take everyone with you. Our bosses, of course, couldn't show the rest of the civilians that our home is possibly failing and falling apart. They are sending us through the service entrance to hide it from everyone. What will suck even more is if any one of us is called into the "experiment" while here, we all have to stop, leave, and come back later to fix the ventilation. This is a six-member job to fix. Pray, mentally pray. No one gets called in.

After some time of all of us debating on who should go up first, I jumped up, wanting to get this over with.

"I'll go first," I shout over the continual arguing.

"Riley, what are you doing? You don't know what the situation is up there. What if..." Will states and then stops. "What if..."

"What if what? The longer we all bicker over who is going up first, the longer the work day takes. I'm going up first, and that's final." I tell him more than anyone else in the group. They are now all looking at us with questioning eyes.

"You all are okay with this since no one seems to be objecting," I say again, and still silence greets me, "Cool."

Gripping hold of the metal bar, I make sure to adjust my air mask - if I should need it - over my shoulders and move my free hand up to grip the bar. Taking the first step up the ladder.

"I'm right behind you," Will calls out, but I don't look back, though I feel a sense of relief knowing he will be right behind me.

Things seem to be going well. As I continue to climb up, we pass the first sector and now the second, and there is only one more to go. I eventually glance downward—I don't recommend that ever— but looking downward, I eventually see the others take their spots on the ladder, with the girl who was with Will following last. I have one more level to go, about twenty-five stairs left, when something catches my shoe, and I slip.

I scream! I frantically grab hold of the bars, gripping the bar tightly as my fingers start to turn white. Due to the added stress, my fingers are starting to slip due to sweat. Do not look down, do not look down. I tell myself.

"Riley, I'm coming! Hang on," a voice calls out below. My head is fuzzy. Focus. Focus. I repeat to myself.

My feet are dangling off the side of the ladder as my hands fight with everything in their power to stay firm on the bars. I feel a body come close to me.

"Riley, can you try to swing your body back on the ladder?" The voice asks. Now, thinking about it, I think it sounds like Will.

"Will?" I questioned.

"Yes, Riley, I'm here," he states, then asks again, "Can you swing your body back onto the ladder?"

"I don't know. I'm scared."

"I know, but you have to try."

Nodding, I try a few attempts to swing my body back on the stairs, with no luck.

"I...I can't."

"Just try again, but when you swing your leg this time, I will grab it and place it on the step, so hold on tight."

"You'll what?" I shout back.

"Just try it."

"Okay..."

I take three deep breaths and start to move my body, pushing my body—swinging it back and forth. Praying my fingers, hold on. When I finally swing close to the step, a hand comes around my ankle, holding me tight. Half of my body slams into the ladder. Letting out a cry, I desperately try not to let my fingers loose from their hold. They are starting to slowly slip. Will's hand, still clasped around my ankle, sends fire surging through my body. A single touch by him is fire. He moves and places my foot on the step, allowing the rest of my body to follow suit. As both of my feet rest on the step, securing my spot on the ladder, I look down to see Will's body cocooning mine. I can feel the heat off his body and his muscles protecting me, shielding me from falling again. Smiling with tears running down my cheeks, I look into his eyes, seeing them full of fear and something else: lust.

"Hey, are you guys okay up there?" Someone shouts up at us, pulling me away from looking at Will's face.

"Yeah," Will shouts down, "only a minor setback. We're okay."

I let out a long breath of air.

"We should continue going up," Will tells me.

"Yeah, yeah," is all I can manage.

After a few very hesitant steps, we make it to the top. I let out a well-needed sigh of relief when he, too, takes a deep breath. I place my right hand on the wall as I bend over, intending on wiping the sweat, dew, or whatever might be on the bottom of my shoe when Will comes right up to me and pushes my head back as his lips connect to mine. Our lips clash together, and we make out at the top of the stairs. His hand comes around my head and pushes me back against the wall. His hand protecting where my head would have smacked the wall.

I taste him as his lips continue to crash with mine. His tongue starts to explore my mouth as his kissing intensifies. His free hand starts to explore over my clothes. I start to feel a longing, a pulsing sensation in my pussy. The wanting, the craving for more. His hand finds my breasts and starts to play with them, but he struggles due to the material of my work clothes. Oh, how I would love to feel him and feel his fingers tease my pussy. If we continue to do these random, surprise make-out sessions, I will have to remember that idea. Will and I make out for what seems like minutes, but in reality, it is only a minute, maybe two, when we hear movement coming from the stairs. Will pulls away and, in doing so, bites my lip. No. No, I want to shout. I don't care who knows, just kiss me, fuck me right here, but unfortunately that doesn't happen.

Will bends down to help the others off the ladder.

"Hey, Riley, that was scary," says one boy from one of the other units.

"Yeah," I reply, my voice cracking.

After finishing work today, we all headed back down to the lunchroom. It's late afternoon, but they are still serving lunch. We fixed the ventilation, and sector three is running smoothly again. I grab my chicken and rice and am about to sit down when my bracelet starts flashing. Of course. Out of habit, I glance over to Will, hoping his bracelet will start flashing too, but nothing happens. He sees my disappointment and shrugs. Smiling, I grab my tray, say bye to everyone, and head down the hallway.

Knocking on the black door, I'm surprised when a male opens it.

"Hi?" I ask.

"Hey there, good-looking," he replies with a wink.

Oh, great, we've got a winner.

"Where's the scientist?" I ask, looking around.

"Oh, she had to run a quick errand. She'll be right back in."

"Great." Not in the mood to strip and prepare myself for the scientist, especially not only in front of him. I set my tray off to the side, sit silently on the edge of the bed and wait. Well, try to.

"So, what's your name?" he asks, waggling his eyebrows.

I roll my eyes and tell him. He smiles and says, "That's a cool name. I'm Logan."

"Cool."

Before Logan can say another word, the scientist knocks once and enters the room. "Glad to see you both here. Sorry for the delay, I had to grab some supplies."

Supplies?

"That's cool. Riley and I were getting to know one another. Weren't we?" Logan asks, elbowing me, his eyes fill with mischief.

"Sure thing," I say, sidestepping to avoid another elbow nudge.

"Well, good," the scientist says. "Today, we're going to start with the basics, and depending on how you both perform, we might add more."

Logan glances at me and winks. "You are going to love my cock," he says, cheeky.

Why don't I recognize Logan? He's been non-stop talking since I entered the room, and yet I don't remember him, ever.

"Logan, what sector are you from?" I interject, cutting off the scientist's instructions.

"What?" He looks genuinely confused.

"I haven't seen you here before. What sector are you from?"

"Oh, I'm actually from a different community," he says, looking away.

A different community? How is that possible?

"Logan is here on a trial basis," the scientist explains, cutting in.

"Trial basis? What does that mean?" I ask, still puzzled.

"If he fits into our program, he'll stay. We'll find him a place to live and work, and then he'll be a part of our "experiments"."

I'm shocked not only because they're adding someone new but

also because he's from an entirely different community. "What did you do to get kicked out of your last community?" I ask, trying to inject some humor into my words.

"Oh honey, wouldn't you like to know?" he replies with a smirk.

"Yes, that's why I'm asking," I say bluntly.

"Maybe I'll tell you during our scene, or what do you call it? An "experiment"?"

My face flushes with heat.

"Okay, good, we've got the introductions out of the way. Now it's time to strip," the scientist says, clearing her throat. "Riley, you'll start on the bed towards the edge. Keep your legs up and close to your body. Logan, you'll stand in front of her."

"Okay..." I say nervously.

Logan doesn't say anything, just smiles.

"Let's get started," the scientist says.

I'm uncomfortable about stripping in front of both of them. After I undress and walk around the privacy curtain, I come to a halt.

HOLY SHIT! Logan's dick is huge, not specifically in length but in width. Fuck, I don't know if I will be able to take that. What do they feed the boys in the other communities?

"You like what you see, darling?" Logan comments, his arrogance coming back in full swing.

"I...I...Um..." I'm speechless.

"Okay, Riley, please get on the bed," the scientist begins.

I climb onto the bed and mentally brace myself for what's about to happen. FUCK, I'm so not ready for this. I try to position myself in a way that might make it less painful. I brace myself.

"Are you ready for me, baby?" he asks, sending a cringe through me that makes me want to throw up.

"Yeah, how about I pass," I reply instead.

"Are you afraid of my cock? Are you afraid I won't fit in your tiny, little cunt?"

"Have you seen the size of your dick?" I shout. Of course, I'm nervous.

"Don't worry, I'll go slow, though only the first time."

"Okay, now that we've had that fun introduction, go ahead and line yourself up," the scientist states.

Not only is his dick massively thick, but I didn't notice until he was coming towards me that his shoulders are also wide. He looks like a giant linebacker, and I feel like a small mouse.

"Okay, Logan, I want you to start with teasing her clit."

"Oh, but where's the fun in that? I don't know about her, but I'm ready to fuck!"

"You're an arrogant ass," I tell him.

"Oh...do you like ass play? Because I love to take your ass. Unless you're a virgin there, then sign me up for some virgin ass."

Looking towards the scientist, I ask, "Can I switch partners?" I can tell she empathizes with me, but she shakes her head and replies in a solemn tone, "Sorry, honey, once you're matched with the partner of the day, you can't switch."

I knew this would be true, but it couldn't hurt to ask. Taking a deep breath, "If you're not gonna tease my clit, I'll do it myself."

"That'll work," he says, "while you do that, I'll stroke my cock and let the pre-cum fall on you, or better yet, I'll let you swallow it."

"Eww, who says those things?"

"That's one of the levels at my former community," he smiles.

"What?"

"Okay," the scientist jumps up from her chair and claps her

hands. Let's start the experiment," purposely cutting off his story.

My mind is racing with curiosity about what he revealed about his former community. Clearly, it was something he wasn't supposed to mention, and the scientist is aware of it.

"Are you ready to take my giant cock?"

"Ew, stop whatever you're saying. I don't know what you did at your former community, but that's not how we do things here."

"Oh... You'll learn, eventually."

"No, I won't."

He gives me a cheeky smile.

Rolling my eyes, I start to rub my clit, getting myself prepared, as he starts stroking his cock.

After a few minutes go by, I feel myself getting wet. I looked down to see that not only has his dick enlarged, but now, it has grown in length. My nerves shoot through the roof, there's no way that thing is gonna fit in my pussy!

"Are you both ready?" The scientist asks cheerfully.

"Oh, I'm ready to fuck her until she is sore."

"Seriously, you need to stop with that talk."

"Okay, before you insert yourself into her, I have a gift for you, Logan," the scientist states, smiling, as she reaches into the unmarked bag she brought.

We both glance at her in confusion. She holds up a large bottle—one I've only seen in school and in the movies they had us watch.

"Oh, fuck, no! There's no way I'm using that shit. She'll get wet just from my cock."

"Is that...?" I question.

"Oh honey, this is lube. It'll help make it...easier for him to

45

insert himself. Logan, she hasn't had anyone quite as large as you."

"Oh, so I'm your first giant, huh?"

I roll my eyes.

"You need to quit rolling your eyes. It only makes me harder."

I roll them again out of spite. "Here you go, Logan," the scientist says, handing him the bottle. "Make sure you use plenty of it. I have more if you need."

"Yeah, we'll use the amount as I think is necessary. I want her screaming as she takes my cock!"

Taking the bottle of lube, Logan squeezes out a hefty amount of lube, rubbing it up and down his shaft. He takes a step closer to me, causing me to freeze with anxiety about what's coming. As I attempt to back up, he growls, "Hold still, will you?"

"What are you doing?"

"I have to put some lube in your pussy."

"In?" I question.

Still nervous, I let him proceed. He slides two of his large fingers with a massive amount of lube to the entrance of my pussy. His fingertips start to rub the outer side of my folds; he surprises me when he shoves them in aggressively. I hold in a moan. He begins to coat the walls of my vagina and try as I might, I can't help, but let a moan escape from my lips.

"Do you like that, baby girl?"

"Seriously," I say, between breaths, "you need to cut out that baby girl shit."

"Hmm," he growls.

I don't know if it's just me feeling his large fingers inside of me, but for a few seconds, I forgot that the scientist in the room was watching our every move.

"I think," I say again, breathlessly, "my vagina is well-lubed now."

"Needy girl, you might need a little bit more lube to be ready to take my cock."

I freeze as my heat flushes through my body, and a clenching feeling begins in my pussy.

"Do you like me talking about my cock? Your pussy twitched when I talked about it," he said.

"No," I snap out.

"Hmm, only time will tell," he continues to coat the walls of my vagina with lube, throwing in some more focused fingering. I attempt to silence a moan and a gasp but fail. Miserably. I hear a low chuckle coming from Logan as he continues moving his fingers around inside me.

I glance over at the scientist, who seems to be in a trance. It takes her a moment to realize I'm staring at her. She shakes her head, clears her throat, and looks down at her clipboard. I can't help but wonder if she's getting off by our interaction.

Logan removes his fingers, as quickly as he inserted them. He puts down the lube bottle and immediately goes back to stroking his cock. My head falls back on the pillow, my eyes focusing on the ceiling tiles. It isn't until I feel the head of his penis at my entrance, do I take a sharp breath, trying to scoot away or off the bed.

"Where are you going?" He asks as he grabs my legs, pulling me back down. "Do I need to tie you?" He chuckles.

Breathlessly, I rise, glaring at him. Before he has a chance to say anything else or for me to think, he knocks the head of his cock, into my folds.

Just from the head of his cock, I can tell how large he is and how much it is going to expand my pussy.

"Take my cock," he growls at me as he pushes in.

Feeling the width of him, my eyes grow wider as a wordless scream comes out of my mouth. Fuck, fuck, FUCK! I glance down to see his cock is only a quarter in. He's not even halfway in, and I'm terrified he's gonna stretch me apart. His cock is way too big for my pussy. I can't help but glance up to see his hazel eyes. There's a devilish glint and something else, something I can't place. Though, I can tell he's enjoying this. Is this more for his pleasure or mine? I truly don't know, sucking in another long, deep breath he pushes further into me. I feel him hit my cervix.

He continues to push in a little further when I desperately gasp, "You...you're far enough in. For God's sake, you've hit my cervix!"

"Well, good, now you know how much of my cock you can take, and now..." he draws out. He bends over so his mouth is next to my ear and whispers—I had to focus to hear him— "One day, I am going to fuck you till you submit."

Surprised and confused, I can feel my eyes widening in shock.

"Now," he says with an evil chuckle as he pulls away, "are you ready?" I fear this is gonna be my only warning.

Unable to move or see anything clearly, I stare at him, frozen in place.

"Well, that's not a no," he remarks and pulls out of me. I'm relieved. To say I was unprepared would be an understatement. He slams back into me. I feel as if I was about to split in half.

He continues to pull out halfway, only to slam back into me. With each thrust, tears begin to fall from my eyes.

We continue for what feels like forever, though I know it's only been a few minutes. Every time he pulls out, I feel a small amount of relief, only to have him slam back into me. I am caught between absolutely hating this and craving more.

I hear a growling sound coming from him. He grips hard onto

my legs as he finishes inside me. He finishes inside me! What? I didn't think the males were allowed to do that.

"Ohh...that was amazing. You have an amazing pussy. Please, I beg you, please let me fuck your ass next time."

"I don't do ass play," I gasp. I'm not sure why I'm so out of breath, but I am panting for air.

Chapter 10

Later that night, I lie in my bed, staring up at my ceiling. Our rooms are small cubes-like spaces. If you have a family, you might have two to three cubes combined into one larger unit. Since it's just me in my cube, I have a small room with a tiny window looking out towards the hall. Most of the walls of the cubes are plain, but after a few years of staring at blank surfaces, I decided to paint the ceiling to avoid the dull, gray expanse.

My mind drifts back to the "experiment" I had earlier today with Logan. I am in physical pain from our "experiment", but it's a feeling I don't necessarily hate.

I hate that guy. I'm not sure why they brought him to our community. I didn't even think that was allowed, but he needs to go back to his original community. Though, it was a change of pace. I'm usually put with...not well-endowed men, aside from Will. Will! Oh my God, I forgot all about him.

Shooting upright in my bed, I realize I completely forgot to check in on Will after our workday. It's not mandatory, but after our intense work day and kiss and close call fuck, it feels necessary. Slipping out of bed, I grab a sweatshirt and put on my shoes before heading out to the commons room. With my mind racing and sleep eluding me, I doubt he'll be in the commons, but there's still a chance.

Walking down the hall, I pass the darkened rooms of my neighbors. I really should be asleep, especially after the day I've had. Pushing forward, I reach the commons and see that Allison is sitting in her usual spot, playing cards again. Scanning the rest of the room, there's no sign of Will or anyone else. Heading over to Allison, I take the spot across from her, wincing when I sit on the hard stool.

"Rough day?" she asks quietly.

"Rough something," I reply, grabbing some cards. Her eyes meet mine with curiosity, but I shake my head and focus on our game.

"What happened today?" she mumbles.

Taking a deep breath, I respond, "Had an "experiment" with a new guy today."

"Oh, another virgin?"

"Nope, he's well experienced."

She shoots a glance up, her eyes meeting mine. They're full of confusion and pure shock. "Are you..." she starts, "are you saying they have a new guy who is not a virgin and who is experienced?"

"Yup," I say, laying down a card.

"How? What?" She stumbles over her words.

"He's from another community," I whisper.

It didn't seem possible that her eyes could have gotten any bigger, but they did right then.

"But..."

"He's from another community. I don't know which one, but he is very experienced."

"How?" she cuts me off.

"I don't know how to answer any of your questions because I have been asking the same ones. All I know is he's here on a trial run. The scientist wouldn't tell me anything else."

She bites her lower lip, no longer interested in the game in front of her.

"What? Do you know something?" I ask.

She only shakes her head, then pauses as if she's contemplating telling me more.

"What?" I urge her.

"There's rumors," she starts, taking a deep breath. "That the "experiments" aren't turning out as expected."

"Meaning?" I ask, confused. "I know we talked about this before, but why are they bringing in more people?"

"They want to match the "experimentation" levels of the other communities."

I'm both shocked and confused.

"What do you know about the other communities?" She asks me.

"Not much. Only that we don't associate with them."

"Right, but is there anything else?"

"No. Why?"

Taking in a long, deep breath, she glances around to make sure no one else has entered the room. Then she begins, "Okay, a few years ago, our community started declining. I'm sure you've noticed it in your job. To survive, we needed to get more funding from the government, and the only way to do that was to prove that our "experiments" were successful. Since the community began, we've been following the same procedures and getting the same results each time—occasionally with a small variation. That's why they've started altering the "experiments" and why you, for example, have been assigned to new ones.

I absorb her words, processing what she told me.

"But now, the rumor that is floating around is that the government still isn't satisfied with our "experiments." They've given us five months to make a change. We've had too many unauthorized sex reports, and our statistics are way down, even with the new "experiments". I wonder if that is why they pulled someone else in from another community."

We're both silent for a while.

"So," she starts, "how was he?"

"What?"

"How was the new guy from the other community?"

I can feel my face flushing. "Oh, that good?" she asks with a smile.

"No, well, yes, but he was a complete ass. I don't know how they run things in the other communities, but the things he said to me."

"What did he say?"

"He called me 'baby girl', asked if I needed to be tied up, said he'd fuck me till I submit and wanted to know if I'll do ass play. He was talking to me as if I were just a thing rather than a person he was with."

Looking up, I see Allison is watching me intently, absorbing my words.

"Allison?" I ask, "Are you okay?"

Clearing her throat, she said, "Oh, yes. Can I ask how big he was?"

"Do girls normally talk about this stuff?" I ask instead.

"Sometimes, yes. In the Old World, definitely."

"Oh, well...he was large."

Her eyes widen. "How...large?"

"Well, I didn't measure, but he was large in both length and width."

"What?" she asks, more shocked than curious.

"Yeah, and with the way he was talking, maybe if I liked that talk, I would have been more turned on, but..."

"But...? Wait, you liked it?"

"No," I shoot back at her.

"Yes, you did. You won't admit it, but you liked it."

"No, no, no," I repeat, though thinking back on it now, some of the words I initially cringed at are starting to stir something within me. I won't give her the satisfaction of admitting she's right, at least not entirely.

"Riley? Are you okay? You disappeared on me."

Shaking my head to clear the thoughts, I said, "No, I'm here. What were you asking?"

"I asked if you'll be seeing him again soon."

"Ew, I don't know, nor do I want to."

"Sure," she says with a smirk.

A few minutes after our conversation, I head back to my room. As I lie there, my mind is racing. Did I like it? His words? I'm not sure. I don't think so, but...maybe.

Deciding to distract my brain, I try to exhaust my body. I reach down into my pants and start to rub my clit. My clit and pussy are still sore from earlier, but it feels good to ease the pain. Feeling the tingling sensation beginning to fill my body as my mind flashes between Logan with his rough fucking and Will with his reassuring, gentle fucking. Two boys, who have been the only ones—seem to be able to pleasure me correctly—even though they are two different experiences.

Chapter 11

The next morning, I woke up to find Will waiting at my door.

"Hey, how'd your "experiment" go?"

No hello, no good morning—just straight to the point.

I blush and try to hide it behind my hair as I turn around to lock the door. There are no valuables in my home, but I lock it as a force of habit.

"It was fine. They're working on creating new "experiments"." I say as I turn back around.

"Really? How so?" he asks as we start heading down the hall to work.

"Yeah, they brought in a new guy from another community."

"Wait, they did what?" He asks, stopping short.

"I had to partner up with another guy from a different community. He didn't specify which community, but he's not from ours."

"Why do you say that?"

I blush again at the thought of Logan's words.

"Let's just say they do things differently in other communities."

"Why aren't you telling me anything? I want to know, I won't tell anyone, I promise. Please..."

"Ugh, okay." I look around and pull him aside. "He...he talked to me in a really strange way."

"Strange" he interjects.

"Yeah," I continue, as in sexual but it was cringey and disgusting. I think, but I don't tell him that.

"Like what? You can't leave me hanging like that."

Taking a deep breath, I recount what I told Allison. As I describe the situation, Will's expression remains neutral, but it shifts slightly when I mention the details. "He fucked me rough and hard. His cock...stretched me." This feels weird to talk about. "He talked to me like an object more than a person he was fucking."

"Oh," was all he said before continuing down the hall.

"Hey, where are you going?" I ask, hurrying to catch up.

"Did you like that?"

"No," I respond.

"Okay."

"What's the matter?"

"Nothing. I just didn't expect you to like it."

"I just told you I didn't."

"Yeah, but your face says otherwise."

"Oh. Wait, why does it matter to you?"

"Wow! I'm sorry, I thought..."

"Thought what?"

"It's nothing."

"No, tell me!"

He continues walking, I grab his arm and pull him back. "What is going on?"

"Riley..." he pauses, clearly conflicted, "I like you." He shouts at me, "And to be honest, I thought you liked me too. But now that you liked what that guy did to you, I know I could never give you that. I thought our kiss at work yesterday meant something."

"Oh," I say, stunned.

"Yeah."

"It did," I say softly.

"You're just saying that."

"No, I'm serious."

"Whatever. We're going to be late for work."

"Will, stop!" I shout, as he continues to walk. "Will!" I grab hold of him, standing on my tiptoes, and kiss him. Our lips connect and an electric current flows through our bodies, fusing us together. I notice people walking past, but I'm too absorbed in the moment to care.

Relationships aren't ideal, due to jealousy and the "experiments", but it's not forbidden. We kiss, until someone bumps into us, breaking us apart.

Chapter 12

A body collides with us, breaking our kiss apart.

"Hey, can I join?" a mysterious voice asks.

Will pulls away from me, biting his lip and shooting a glaring look at the intruder. "Excuse me?"

"That looks like fun, can I join?" That voice, sounds familiar, but how? Then it dawns on me. No!

"Please leave," Will sternly asks.

"How about, no."

"I'm only going to ask once more. We're having a moment."

"Yes, I can see that," the voice responds, "which is why I'm asking. Tell him, Riley. How good I fucked you the other day and how much you want more of my cock."

LOGAN!

"Fuck," slips past my lips.

"Now, you remember me," he says, grinning. "Hi, I'm Logan King," he extends his hand to shake hands with Will. Will just stands there, continuing to glare at Logan.

"No handshake? Okay, anyway Riley, I was coming to find you."

"Me?" I ask, confused.

"I was given the option to pick my next partner for the next experiment, and I want to ask you. Since we had a lot of fun, I want you, so we can continue what we started."

A shiver runs down my spine. I back away from Logan, positioning Will between us.

"Come on, baby, it was fun. I bet your pussy is begging for my cock again. I bet this guy can't match mine." He grins, with his cocky smile.

"Who the fuck are you?" Will asks, gritting his teeth together. "You need to back the fuck up."

I didn't know Will had a pissed-off side or even a protective mode. Right now, he's acting like my bodyguard—or maybe even my boyfriend. We just admitted we liked one another, does this mean he's my boyfriend? I'm not sure what to make of it.

"I'm Logan," he continues, "I already tried to introduce myself. Riley and I here had our "experiment" yesterday, where I fucked her good and hard. Which she enjoyed and like I said, I've been given the option to choose my next partner and I want her."

"That's not going to happen." Will grits out. "And how are you even allowed to pick your partner, that is not how the "experiments" work. The scientists select our partners for us."

Logan begins shaking his head. "Nope, not anymore. New rules. The people with the highest statistics can pick who they want to partner up with."

Is that true? Can it be? We can pick who we want to partner up with now? Is this because of the changes they are making? It has to be, right?

"Riley, come on, let's go. I have to get to the "experiment" room." Logan attempts to grab my arm.

"No," I spit out, still behind Will.

"See, she doesn't want to partner with you."

"Riley, come on. I can go slower if you're too scared."

"I'm...I'm not scared, I just don't like you. Meaning if I'm not required, I don't want to be paired with you."

Logan doesn't say or do anything else. Only stares at me with disbelief and a hint of anger. "Fine," he says after a long moment, then continues to walk away, fist clenched at his sides.

When Logan finally turns the corner, Will starts talking first, "Well...that was weird."

"Yeah, you're telling me. I don't want to be paired with him. I was fearing he would split me in half."

Will shoots a look at me. Shaking my head I decide not to elaborate. "Come on, we are probably extremely late for work now."

"You're probably right." Will grabs my hand as we walk down the hall together.

Boyfriend, check. Yes, I would consider him my boyfriend.

Chapter 13

Work began and ended without much excitement. I had to fix a few things for the farmers and the scientists, but nothing out of the ordinary. At the end of the day, Will walked me back to my room. His original plan was to escort me back and then head out for dinner— his brother wanted to meet with him tonight for dinner—or at least that was his original plan.

As soon as I opened the door to my cube, Will tackled me to my bed, where we ended up making out. His hands caressed my chin and then explored under my shirt. Found out something new about myself, I like...no love it when he squeezes my breast, especially my nipples. I love the fact we can make out on my bed with no one able to interrupt us.

It was Will who had to slow me down when I wanted to start removing clothes after his hand found its way to my breasts and nipples. I attempted to take off my shirt, but he broke the spell. Will cleared his throat and quickly removed his hand from my chest. I let out a sign of disbelief.

"Sorry," he said, "we should stop. We don't want anything to happen that would cause us to get into trouble."

He was right, of course, but I still wanted to go further.

We decided to head to dinner together. He met up with his brother there too. When they're off talking about their work, my mind wanders off to the altercation between Will and Logan this morning.

My mind pulls me out of my thoughts when my name is being called.

"Riley. Hey, Riley!"

"What?" I ask, as though I just woke up. I guess I did in a way.

"Your bracelet."

"What?" I ask again.

"Your bracelet is not only flashing but beeping, and has been for a few minutes now."

"Oh, shit." Tapping the button, indicating 'I'm on my way,' I finish up my dinner and head to the "experiment" room.

On my way, I bumped into two girls I was in school with a few years ago. They were giggling at one another, but one girl had a bruise forming on her wrist.

"Hey, Ashley. Are you okay?" I stop and gesture to her wrist.

She lets out another round of giggles. "Oh, yes," she says.

"What happened?" I can't seem to let it slide. No one should have bruises like that. It looks like someone grabbed her and didn't let go.

"Oh," she looks down at it again, "it was from the "experiment". I met a new boy who loves to be rough, really rough," she blushes out of control. "He must have grabbed too hard on my wrist," she starts giggling again.

My whole body heats up and a sickening feeling sets in my stomach. I know exactly who she partnered up with.

Logan.

After knocking on the door and entering the room. I'm shocked when I see Logan. I really shouldn't be shocked anymore. If the girl I passed was telling the truth that the new guy is Logan and did partner with her then he shouldn't be in the rotation for a few days, or even a week. Why is he here now? And wait? There's another male figure here, too. It isn't until the other male figure turns around, do I see it's Will. What? I feel faint.

"Will? Logan?" I ask, "What are you both doing here?"

"I..." Will starts, but Logan cuts him off, "I called you both here."

"You? Did you call us? How?" I am confused.

"Yes," he says, with an evil smile.

"How? Why?" Will and I ask, in unison.

"Well, I got to thinking," he starts, but I cut him off.

"Wait, how are you able to experiment today, didn't you pair with someone yesterday?"

"Yes, how did you know that? Have you been checking up on me? Wait, are you jealous? Oh, you are." He grins.

"One, not jealous, and two, saw a girl with bruises and she said she got it from the new guy. So far you are the only new guy in our community, who's NOT a virgin."

"So, you have been checking up on me. You are jealous. Did you get a weird gut feeling when she told you?" He asks.

I didn't answer him. Didn't want to admit he was right, but at the same time, no I'm not jealous. I was worried about that girl, but I didn't answer quickly enough. He takes that as my answer.

Logan lets out a long, bit of chuckles. "Oh, this will be fun."

I had forgotten that Will was in the room until he walked in front of me.

"Riley?" Will asks. "Were you?"

"Was I what?" I snap without meaning to.

"Jealous?"

"No! I wasn't jealous, I was worried about that girl's safety. She had bright-colored bruises along her wrist. I was worried she was attacked or beaten."

"Oh, she enjoyed her punishment," Logan says, choosing his words carefully.

"Punishment? No, I don't want to know." I say, "What are we all doing here?" I ask instead.

"Ah, yes," Logan starts, "I was able to convince the scientist, I needed a while to look over my statistics, alone. Then, I proceeded to hack the computer into sending an alert to you both. Will, it is time to be a man and Riley, you going to learn to enjoy it, like every female should."

Will and I stare at Logan as if he had just grown three heads. "What?" We ask in unison.

"I'm going to teach you both how to have sex, and not just ordinary sex, but rough, fun sex."

Chapter 14

Logan, Will, and I stare at one another, unsure who should move first. I'm sure Logan would take the first step eventually, but no one moves.

"I'm sorry, you're what? Going to teach us how to have sex?" I ask.

"Yes! Fun sex," Logan answers.

"Fun sex? Is that what you called our "experiment" the other day? Fun?"

"Oh, was it not fun for you?"

"No! I was in pain afterward, and the way you were talking to me made me feel disgusted."

"You liked it," a small, barely a whisper came from Will's direction.

"What?" I say at the same time as Logan says, "See, I knew you liked it!"

"Will, I didn't. Or I'm trying not to. That's not me," I plead with him.

"Logan?" Will calmly asks, "Teach me to fuck like you. I want her to enjoy herself, but I still want to be...me."

Logan's smile is so large, that one would think he was granted access to the largest candy store ever. As if this is his favorite day of his life. "With pleasure," he remarks.

Chapter 15

Well, things went differently than I expected. After stripping and laying down on the bed, Will first attempted to be direct with me, but failed. Logan decided to take over and now, here we are. I am currently pinned down, with Logan's hands firmly wrapped around my wrist and his legs pressing my legs to the bed. At one point, his right-hand leaves my wrist, but his elbow comes down in its place, and his now-free hand wraps around my neck. He's not cutting off air, just giving me the sensation of being choked.

His body leans over me, and I can smell his cologne. The placement of his body over mine ignites a spark in me. He leans down close to my ear and whispers, "I wasn't happy you turned me down. I had to find a small bunny to take your place, but now that I have permission to show how you should be fucked, I'm going to take that opportunity and fuck your tight, wet pussy. Don't worry, I'll go slow at first, so your little golden retriever, over there," —my eyes dart over to Will, who is watching us. He can't hear what Logan is saying, but he is at the edge of his seat waiting— "Yes, good girl, watch your golden retriever puppy while I fuck you and fuck you HARD!"

I gulp, unsure of what I'm swallowing since my mouth is dry and my head is spinning with confusion and excitement.

"Are you ready...?" Logan begins. I can tell he wanted to add a pet name but stopped himself. "What do you want to be called during this scene?" he asks me.

"What?" I ask, my voice trembling slightly.

"Pick a name. A nickname. A pet name."

"Oh, I don't know."

"Is there anything I've said so far you like?"

I bite my lip and glance at Will.

"He can't help you, darling," his hand grabs my chin, turning my head back to face him. "You have to pick something I can use," as his hand moves back down to my throat, a little tighter.

"Darling or good girl works," I whisper.

"Okay, I can work with that. Are you ready, darling?" He continues as he stretches out the last part of "darling," his warm breath sends goosebumps across my skin.

I sneak a glance back at Will, I nod slowly, trying not to reveal my eagerness too much.

"Good!" he growls. Without realizing it, he has since removed his hand from my throat and is now moving it south. Dragging his fingers down my neck to the line between my breasts, barely touching me but still making contact with my skin.

I take in a sharp breath as his fingers trail off course towards my breasts, first circling my left breast, creating a spiral circle closing in to pinch my nipple. A sensation fills my pussy. He quickly takes his fingers off my nipple as I let out a gasp. He bends over, connecting his mouth to my nipple. He blows out a puff of air, making my nipple harden. I arch my back in response. Logan's fingers start tracing my right breast and nipple, but still conscious that his mouth is on my left breast. Circling my right nipple with his tongue. He bites down on my left one, and I let out a sharp breath and moan louder than I think I have ever moaned. The sensations, feeling his hand play with my right nipple, his teeth lightly biting my left one again. Oh my god!

Logan continues his torture for a little bit longer, adding squeezes to my breasts. My eyes closed as my body took in all the sensations. A shiver runs down my body as more tingling sensations fill my pussy. Logan releases his hand and his mouth from my breasts and starts to move his finger drag down, continuing on its original route. I arch my back when he reaches my hips. He traces along my waistline, bucking my hips upward out of expectation.

"Hmm, a little greedy? Darling?" Logan growls.

I moan in response as Logan lets out a small chuckle.

"Will, come here," Logan says.

My head falls to the side, and I watch Will stand from his seat and walk over.

"Now, Will, I have gotten her started. I'm going to have you jump in, but then I will take over again in a bit," Logan says as he moves around the bed and grabs hold of my wrists, moving them above my head, using his weight to hold me down.

"Okay," Will says breathlessly, "what do you want me to do?"

"Continue following the trail down to her pussy with your finger. Don't insert it yet, but tease her," he smiles. "Tease her like her life depends on it."

Will looks up and meets Logan's eyes. They both nod to one another.

"Will," I say, but he cuts me off by continuing the trail of tinglings. He grips my hips, suddenly pulling me forward close to the edge of the bed. My hands are still held in place by Logan's weight, stretching my body between the two boys. Will bends over and whispers in my ear, "You're mine. He may fuck you, teach me how to fuck you, but you're mine. You hear me?" He doesn't let me respond, only leans back up and starts teasing me by putting the head of his cock at my entrance. I know Logan said to tease me, but this is cruel. My whole body can't handle everything. I want...no need for someone to fuck me. I don't care which one, somebody fuck me.

Will continues to rub his cock up and down my entrance, but instead of inserting it as I hope, he removes his cock and starts rubbing my clit.

I moan, loudly while bucking my hips, hoping something might accidentally slip in. No, luck. Instead, Logan leans over, "What are you attempting to do, darling?"

"Nothing," I smile.

"Are you wanting our cocks?"

I moan while nodding, "Please!" I beg.

"Will," Logan begins, "how close do you think she is?"

Will looks at me, and I can tell he's trying to maintain a stern, mean demeanor, but I can see that he's enjoying himself.

"Will, please," I beg again, "fuck me!"

"Hmm, I don't think you're close. I should tease you a bit more."

"No...please," Looking upward toward Logan, I desperately plead, "Please, Logan fuck me!"

Will's head shoots up, "So because I won't fuck you, you turn to him?" he growls, he's angry now. I swallow the excess saliva in my mouth.

"Will..." I start, in response, Will shoots his hand forward covering my mouth. "No talking!" he spits out.

His free hand comes back to my clit and circles it roughly. I moan and scream into his hand. No, I feel as if I will explode. I am moving my hips up and down, Will's body holds my legs in place, similar to how Logan's body pinned me down. I can't move, I can only take what he is giving me. My fingers attempt to grab at anything, with no luck. They are still pinned above my head, head down by Logan's weight.

I am still screaming in Will's hand when he jumps off the bed. The cold air hits my now exposed skin as he abruptly gets off the bed. Leaving me exposed and still being pinned down by Logan.

Chapter 16

"Where are you going, dude? You okay?" Logan asks.

"Yeah, I need a minute," Will responds.

"Okay, I don't want to rush you, but she will need a release, so don't wait too long."

"I know, I know. Give me a minute."

"Do you want me to take over?"

"NO!" Will snaps. Logan's grip tightens on my wrists. I watch his breaths, they are labored, he was full into the scene and now isn't sure what is going on.

Will moves and grabs one of the drawers in the room, yanking the drawer open, and pulling out a bottle of lube and a condom wrapper. Both Logan and I inhale a deep breath. I know that I will need more touching soon, or I will lose this feeling. I feel Logan's soft touches grazing up and down my arm as he continues to hold me firmly to the bed.

Will comes forward. "I'm sorry, I was about to come, but this is new to me. I couldn't control how it was affecting me."

"What were you feeling?" Logan asks Will.

"I wanted to dominate you, Riley. Do things I never could have imagined doing."

"Good. That's good."

"What?"

"When I get into a "scene" that is how I feel and I use that as fuel."

Logan is actually... caring—is that the right word? I'm not sure.

I am lost in my thoughts for a few minutes, but I am abruptly pulled back when I hear the sound of air escaping from the lube bottle. I look down to see Will has put on the condom and is now squirting a handful of lube onto his fingers. He moves his fingers to my pussy and starts rubbing my clit, dragging the lube to my lips, and shoving his fingers into my pussy. I gasp, attempting to sit upright, only to remember Logan's holding onto my wrists. A whimper leaves my lips, as my hips start their movements again.

"Will..." I breathlessly say, "fu...fuck me! Please, I'm begging you. Shove your cock in me."

"Patience," he says, back in his control dementor.

"We might need more lube!" Logan says with a chuckle.

A few more strokes of his fingers along my lips and in my pussy, does he finally insert his cock. His fingers are still in my pussy. I have both his cock and fingers in my pussy, stretching me. I scream in pain and lust!

Will removes his finger leaving his cock inside me. He moves his covered fingers from my wetness to my mouth.

"Suck," he says.

Unsure of what else to do, I listen to him, I suck his fingers, tasting me off his fingers. I moan, as his fingers are still inside my mouth.

He yanks his fingers out of my mouth and I lick my lips, still tasting my wetness on my lips.

He fucks me with his cock, harder than he did the last time we were in this room. I love feeling him inside me. He fucks me hard, slamming into me, holding onto my legs for dear life. I hear Will and Logan talking, but I'm so drawn into my pleasure, that I don't understand what they are saying until I feel Logan's hand releasing from my wrist and tilting my chin upward.

When did Logan get on the bed? He is now sitting above my head, still pinning my wrists above my head, but with his legs.

Logan moves my chin on an angle and moves to his knees.

He's not gonna do what I think he is, is he? Oh my god...!

Will continues to pound hard into my pussy, I'm so close to coming. Logan is now stroking his cock, quickly, moaning to himself. I wet my lips, mentally preparing myself. I try to move my arms, only to find they're pinned down with his legs.

Logan groans as he grips my chin, holding it in place, and shoves his cock into my mouth. I gag, only for Logan to shove his cock deeper into my mouth as he starts to fuck my mouth.

I have two boys fucking me. My mouth and my pussy. I feel my body rocking back and forth. A moan tries to escape my lips, only to vibrate against Logan's hard, giant cock. He groans in response, gripping my neck. Now, I desperately need to moan, scream, and release the sound of pleasure, but I am unable to.

Chapter 17

Logan and Will fuck me till I am senseless. By the time we all finished, Will and I finishing as he was fucking me, and Logan fucking my mouth until he came. I have no energy. I couldn't even think about moving my arm. Will took care of the aftercare as Logan cleaned up the room.

When we were done in the room, Will carried me back to my room. I'm shocked there wasn't anyone in the hallways. Dinner should have been letting out, right? Or did we spend more time there than I thought?

Will helped me get dressed for bed and laid down next to me for a while. When morning came, I found my bed empty of him.

Getting up to attempt to start the day, when I realize just how sore I am, deciding it might be best to call in, I lay back down and message my boss. When I got the "okay" message from him, I turned around and went back to bed.

I'm awoken a few hours later when my room door is being forced inward.

"What is happening!" I shout, jumping upward.

"Riley Reyes?" They ask, sternly.

"Yes," I say, nervous.

"You have violated the unauthorized sex law, and you will be terminated from your job here and sent to Community Two."

Chapter 18

Will

Laying in bed, I rethink what we all just did. The three of us. Not only Riley and I, but Riley, Logan, and I. The three of us didn't just break the law. No, we broke the law by having an unmonitored, unauthorized threesome. What did Logan call it? Double Penetration?

I have a new sense of meaning now. It's a feeling similar to adrenaline, but not. That's not the right word? A sensation? No belonging? Maybe. Oh, I'm not sure, but I have a new thought of how things can be.

I don't have to be this golden retriever boyfriend if Riley still thinks of me as her boyfriend. I can and want to be more, more like Logan. The power he holds. The demanding influence he holds over Riley. I'm not sure what causes it, but I know I want it. I want to be able to harness that talent. That ability.

I wonder if Riley liked how things played out. Did she like me fucking her pussy, while Logan fucked her mouth? I wonder if she'd let us, men, reverse roles next time? I would love for her mouth to be around my cock.

I move my hand down to my sweatpants waistband, as the image of her red lips, sucking my cock till I come. When my hand slips under the band, a knock sounds on the door. A tingly happy feeling fills my body.

"Riley?" I say before I have a chance to think. Maybe she is here to see me. Maybe she wishes we got to cuddle after our fun. Or maybe she wants another round. I'd be happy to give her anything.

Removing my hand from my waistband, I slide my legs over, pulling myself upwards.

Another knock sounds, "Riley, you know you don't have to knock. You can just come in."

The doorknob turns, but my excitement falls short when men, soldiers, walk through the door. "Who are you?" I question, stopping short.

"Will Davis?"

"Yes?"

"You have violated the unauthorized sex law, and you will be terminated from your job here and sent to Community Two."

I turn towards my desk, unsure what to do or where to run. When a painful pinch comes at the base of my neck. Glancing at my small mirror dangling on the wall to the right of me– I see one of the soldiers has stabbed me with a needle. A second later, I feel my body collapse to the floor as my vision goes dark.

The End.

www.ingramcontent.com/pod-product-compliance
Lightning Source LLC
Chambersburg PA
CBHW071542100726
47908CB00004B/1479